The Altos

Like "The Sopranos" only Lower!
An Interactive Comic Mystery

by

David Landau

Music & Lyrics by

Nikki Stern

SAMUEL FRENCH

FOUNDED 1830

NEW YORK HOLLYWOOD LONDON TORONTO

SAMUELFRENCH.COM

IMPORTANT BILLING AND CREDIT
REQUIREMENTS

All producers of *THE ALTOS* *must* give credit to the Author of the Play in all programs distributed in connection with performances of the Play, and in all instances in which the title of the Play appears for the purposes of advertising, publicizing or otherwise exploiting the Play and/or a production. The name of the Author *must* appear on a separate line on which no other name appears, immediately following the title and *must* appear in size of type not less than fifty percent of the size of the title type.

THE ALTOS: LIKE THE SOPRANOS ONLY LOWER first opened in May 2001 at the Murder to Go Dinner Theatre in Cedar Knolls, NJ under the direction of David Landau with the following cast;

TONY ALTO . . . . .Joe Molino
TOFFEE ALTO . . . . Kathryn Smizer
CHRIS . . . . Peter Timony
UNCLE SENIOR . . . . Bob Lowy
NONA . . . . Gayle Hendricks
DR. MALAISE . . . . .Antoinette Doherty

INTRODUCTION

I invented the interactive mystery play back in the early 1980s as an attempt to mix environmental theater with audience involvement. My goal was to allow the audience to experience the story as if they were extras in a movie. The entire production, from script to props, direction to surroundings, was oriented towards encompassing the audience in the world of the mystery and not merely with the game of solving it. Mystery parlor games existed since the turn of the century. As theater, it is the story of the characters which must always take center stage - a story of people who find themselves in desperate situations and are compelled to perform desperate acts. The comedy must come from the characters and not at their expense or that of the story.

It can become tempting for cast members to play for a laugh, but this seldom works. The audience laughs the most at things that are played straight - discovering the humor for themselves. Audiences identify and sympathize with characters that are real and seldom with caricatures. An actor's approach to an interactive mystery should be no different than that taken to Shakespeare or any other theatrical work. Why is the character there, what are they thinking, why are they doing what they do and what do they want? The more real, the more the audience becomes involved in this new reality and the more both they and the performers will enjoy the experience. The audience itself is utilized by the performer as a prop, a confidant, another cast member. The audience is on stage with them.

In a true mystery there can be only one logical culprit, pointed out not only by the clues, but by the motivation, personality and situation that character finds himself/herself in. While there are a number of other likely suspects, this character is the inevitable guilty party. The mystery has been sown well when the average of correct guesses is 10 - 20%. By the end of the play, when all is revealed, the audience should sigh a collective 'Of course, I should have thought of that!'

The interactive mystery play offers theater patrons, performers and producers many unique opportunities. The audience can be taken to the edge with suspense and then suddenly dropped into a humorous release of tension. The characters can become so real that they can reach out and touch the audience, literally. The theatrical fourth wall is placed behind the audience. If done correctly, the interactive play can be one of the most involving forms of theater possible.

David Landau
Creator of the first interactive mystery play, *The Mystery Express,*
Dec. 1982
Member of The Dramatists Guild and Mystery Writers of America

NOTES ON PRODUCTION

PERFORMANCE SPACE

The following play was designed to be performed in a dining room, dinner theater, night club, theater-in-the-round, or a thrust stage where the acting area is level with the first row. The intention is to make the audience feel like they are actually in the location of the story. The performance is a sort of reverse theater in the round, with action performed around the circumference of the seating area, as well as down the aisles and in the center. The audience should be seated at tables, either dinner or cocktail. Tables could be added in font of the first row in the case of thrust or arena stages. Audience members can also be seated on stage.

SCENES & BREAKS

The script is formatted into four or five scenes running in length from 12 to 20 minutes. Between each scene is time to serve a course of a meal, serve drinks, or play music as desired. During these breaks characters mingle helping to establish character and reveal information to the audience in a one on one manner. The script can easily be adapted to eliminate some of these breaks. If this is the desire, black-outs should take place between scenes, with an intermission between either scenes 2 and 3 (if four scenes) or 3 and 4 (if five scenes). There should be some kind of break just before the finale scene to allow audience members to hand in their guesses as to 'whodunit'.

MUSICAL NUMBERS

The musical numbers in the show have been designed to be performed to a taped play back. Once a performance license has been secured, an audio tape with recordings of both the instrumentals and the composer singing the lyrics can be obtained from Samuel French. Also on the tape is the opening theme music which is to be used at the beginning of each scene.

For more information contact Samuel French, Inc. at info@samuel-french.com.

Music & Lyrics were composed by Nikki Stern.

AWARDING PRIZES

The 'Sleuth Sheets' are handed out with the programs at the beginning of the night and collected by the characters before the finale scene. They should be handed to the stage manager, who will sort out the correct answers. After the curtain call, the correct answers are handed to the main character, who reads out the names of the successful sleuths. Generally, all correct answers are placed in a hat and a character draws one name. A prize is then awarded to that patron by a cast member. The prize can be a bottle of wine, a t-shirt, almost anything. It's the thought that counts.

CAST

TONY ALTO	A local boss who runs a strip club as a cover
TOFFEE ALTO	His wife, who has the hots for her priest
CHRIS	His incompetent nephew, wants to be a made-man and a Hollywood star
UNCLE SENIOR	Under indictment, hates Tony and wants to run things, wears numerous police collars, bracelets, anklets.
NONA	His mother, who hates him for trying to send her to a home
DR. MALAISE	his shrink
FATHER FLIP	has the hots for Toffee
DELIVERY MAN/HITMAN	same actor as Father Flip

SETTING

Tony's funeral. There is an urn and a photo of Tony by a funeral wreath. On the tables are newspapers with a story about mobster Tony Alto being blown up in his car. Programs are invites to the wake, with sleuth sheets inside asking "Who wants Tony dead? Why? How many titles of gangster movies & TV shows are in the show?"

Chris greets everyone at the door, asking them to check their weapons. There is a table full of various weapons - guns, knifes, nun-chucks, swords, etc. Occasionally he'll 'pull' a weapon out of a man's jacket or from a woman's coat and add them to the pile. He recognizes people as fellow gangsters.

Father and Toffee seat guests, thanking them for coming. Uncle Senior and Nona mingle.

PRE-SHOW MINGLE

DR. MALAISE - hands out business cards for her practice, saying she specializes in helping people with dubious professions - no questions asked, no answers given.

FATHER - mingles, asking women if they have anything to confess to. If not, he says 'what a shame - would you like to?'

TOFFEE - recognizes people as gangsters

NONA - gets confused, welcomes people to Tony's Wedding. Recognizes people as long dead relatives - then later, doesn't recognize them.

UNCLE SENIOR - recognizes people as gangsters. Tells them that now he's running things so they better be nice to him, show him respect.

CHRIS - recognizes people as fellow gangsters.

All gangster characters introduce themselves to guests and recognize them as fellow gangsters and club dancers with names such as;
"Machine Gun Molly"
"Bennie the Bum"
"Slick Susan"
"Jimmy the Gun"
"Sidney the Schyster - lawyer to the mob"
"Baby Face Nicky"
"Madam Monroe - the runner of the biggest brothel in New York"
"Patricia the Pinch"
"Big Ben"
"Nasty Nell"
"Jimmy, the coachroach"

The opening conversation can be along the lines of:
"How long have you been out of then slammer?"
"I heard you was the trigger on that hit in Brooklyn."
"Didn't I hear you was becoming a priest?"
"Isn't there a contract out on your life?"
"I heard your gang took a dive when Gotti got put away. Where are you hiding out these days?"
"Nice dudes. Ain't that the threads Lucky Louie was wearing when they buried him?"
"Aren't you the Governors daughter?"
"Now I remember where I saw you before - at Badda Bangs. I didn't recognize you with your clothes on."
"Wasn't you working with the Blue Gang in Detroit?"
"Listen, thanks for that hot tip on Blue Bird at Belmont. That horse paid me twelve to one. How'd you know that long shot was going to come in? ... Got any more?"

All characters know that Tony owns Badda Bangs, a men's entertainment dance club.

Scene I

(*Theme music. Lights down, lights up.* **CHRIS** *approaches the urn. He crosses himself.*)

CHRIS. You know, I never thought this time would come, Uncle T. I thought you were invincible. They tried alright, but you kept beatin them. But not this time, huh Uncle T? I was countin on you. I was counting on you making me a made man. But you won't do it. I know I messed up a few times – you was always on my can about that. You never let up on me. Well, I guess you're gonna have to let up on me now, huh?

(**NONA** *approaches.*)

CHRIS. We're gonna find out who it was that done this, Uncle T. You just watch from up – down – wherever you is and you'll see. (*To* **NONA**) I'm sorry Mrs. Alto.

NONA. (*Sobbing*) My son – my only son.

(*As soon as* **CHRIS** *leaves,* **NONA** *stops sobbing.*)

NONA. I guess you can't sell my house out from under me now, can you Tony – huh? See what happen's when you try to take the home away from the one that gave you your life. Let me see you try and force me into a nursing home now, you ungrateful louse.

(**UNCLE SENIOR** *walks up. She starts sobbing again.*)

NONA. My only son – my little boy.

SENIOR. At least its over now, Nona.

NONA. You bite your tongue and choke on it.

(*She leaves. He looks stunned.*)

SENIOR. Well, Tony – we see who really runs things now, don't we. You never had no respect for the old way – the way things were supposed to be. See where it's gotten you now? You're nothin but plant food. You thought you were such a big man. I'm the one gettin indicted, wearing all these stupid electronic collars and bracelets – I set off shoplifter alarms everywhere I go. You did this to me, Tony. Now look where you're at.

(**FATHER** *walks up.*)

SENIOR. Chow, Tony.

FATHER. He will be greatly missed.

SENIOR. He was missed several times, Father. But not this time.

(**SENIOR** *leaves.*)

FATHER. Tony Alto. What didn't you have? God gave you so much to be thankful for, but you abused it. You neglected your beautiful loving wife for power and greed and now look at where it has gotten you. Not even you can keep cheating death.

(**TOFFEE** *joins him.*)

TOFFEE. Oh, Father Flip, thank you so much for all your help and, well, being there for me. I know Tony was never a real church going guy and all. And for you to arrange all this in such a rush on his behalf. I know he'd – I'd –

FATHER. Funerals are for the living, not the departed. How are the children doing?

TOFFEE. Not good. Maybe if you had a word with them? I know you've given me – (*thinking sexual*) your piece – (*catching herself*) I mean some piece – piece of mind – um –

FATHER. Of course, I'm always (*thinking sexual*) at your service in your hours or need.

(*They virtually lust into each others arms. Almost ready to kiss.*)

FATHER. The children.

TOFFEE. The children.

(*They suddenly realize they are being watched and quickly break from one another.*)

FATHER. Where are the children?

TOFFEE. Oh, ah – well, – my daughter Pasture is right here (*pointing out a female guest*) and my son Little Tony (*pointing out a male guest*).

FATHER. Come children.

TOFFEE. (*Encouraging them to go up to him*) Come on you two. The father's here to help us get through this.

(**FATHER** *and* **TOFFEE** *get the two audience people to join them by the urn. They all hold hands.*)

FATHER. I know this is hard for you – as it is hard for your mother. It's always been hard for your mother. – Er – Nothing I say can make up for your loss, so – I won't say anything. But perhaps it would help if you did. Maybe if you each gave us a memory of your father, Tony Alto. You go pasture, being the eldest and his little princess. Tell us your fondest memory of something you did with your father.

(*Who knows what she'll say, if anything. If she doesn't talk,* **TOFFEE** *will say she's over come with grief.*)

FATHER. And now you, Little Tony. The new man of the house and your father's name sake. Tell us a lasting memory of something between you and your father.

(*If he doesn't talk,* **TOFFEE** *will say he has laryngitis from too much crying.*)

FATHER. (*As if leading a prayer*) Though the body may be gone, singed to a crisp and charred beyond recognition in a fiery explosion that transformed his SUV into a giant ashtray – these fine memories will live on, keeping Tony Alto forever in our hearts. Now, doesn't that make things a little better?

TOFFEE. Oh, Father, you always know – (*sexual*) how to make me feel better. – Er, kids go, sit down again and mourn with the rest of the guests.

(*They send the audience members back to their seats.*)

TOFFEE. Oh, God I can't believe she's here.

FATHER. Who?

TOFFEE. That Russian tramp of his – Tony's mistress. She has the nerve to show up here. That's her, right over there. (*Points and describes a woman in the audience*).

FATHER. We must let all pay their last respects.

TOFFEE. I'll make her pay, alright.

(*She storms up to the table, but **CHRIS** stops her.*)

CHRIS. Aunt Toffee, not here, not now – not in front of your kids.

TOFFEE. You're right, Chris. Not yet.

(*She turns and walks away. **CHRIS** turns to the female guest.*)

CHRIS. Hey, now that Tony's gone, I'm gonna be taking over his territory – and you're part of his territory!

SENIOR. What do you mean you're taking over his territory? He don't got no territory. I'm running the show, like I was supposed to running things before. So any thought about territory – forget about it. You little morte e devom.

(**SENIOR** *walks away.* **CHRIS** *pulls out a garage door opener.*)

CHRIS. (*to woman*) My remote garage door opener – watch me make that sfa chem jump.

(*He pushes the garage door opener and suddenly **UNCLE SENIOR** jumps – shocked. During this **TONY**, dressed as a woman in mourning in black shawl and veil has entered. Meanwhile, **DR. MALAISE** has walked up to **TOFFEE**.*)

TOFFEE. Thank you for coming Doc. You don't mind if I call you doc do you? I mean, is that what Tony called you?

MALAISE. You can call me whatever makes you feel comfortable, Mrs. Alto. I'm here for you, not Tony anymore.

TOFFEE. Thank you for the offer, but I don't really need a shrink. I've got Father Flip to keep me going – (*lost in her own thoughts of sexual excitement*) and going and going and going and – (*realizing, composing*) I should be going – er – to talk with the others.

(*As she leaves* **TONY** *whispers to* **MALAISE**.)

TONY. Pssssst.

MALAISE. Excuse me?

TONY. It's me.

MALAISE. Most people I meet don't know who they are.

TONY. I'm Tony, Doc.

MALAISE. You're who?

(**TONY** *takes off the vale.* **MALAISE** *is shocked.*)

TONY. Shhhhh. Don't say nothin.

MALAISE. Anything.

TONY. What?

MALAISE. Don't say anything. Don't say nothin is a double negative, which would mean you wanted me to say something, which is contrary to your true intention.

TONY. Stop that!

MALAISE. And why aren't you dead? I mean, you're supposed to be dead – I mean, why are you letting everyone think that you're dead?

TONY. Cause that bomb was in my car, which means someone was trying to kill me. So If I let everyone think I'm dead, then maybe I'll find out who was the wise guy.

MALAISE. Tony, did you stop taking the lithium when I told you to?

TONY. Listen, Doc – whoever put the hit on me would come to the funeral to gloat – and make sure I was really a done deal. Now I need your help.

MALAISE. Oh, so now you're actually asking me for help. I remember the first time you came to see me. You gave me a real song and dance.

TONY. Oh, yeah. I remember.

(*Lights dim, spot on Tony as he sings hip/hop rap song* ***"RESPECT."***)

TONY. (*Singing*)

I WONDER WHY I'M HERE
I WONDER WHAT I'LL DO
I WONDER HOW TO EXPLAIN MYSELF
TO SOMEONE LIKE YOU

THIS AIN'T THE WAY TO START
I GUESS I SHOULDDA PLANNED
SO WHAT'S THE MODERN LINGO
YOU SHRINKS USE TO UNDERSTAND?

"LISTEN"
(*hip-hop beat starts*)

Now I don't mean to disrespect your profession
But you're not tight with the tradition, cappiche?
But hey, I'm here, And we got, what, an hour?
So I gotta familiarize you With my little niche

Maybe I should start by speaking from the heart
About my view of the way things should be
But I'm not gonna do that, 'cause what you gotta know
Is how hard it is sometimes to be me

I like what I do, but my line of work is tough
You know, things can get rough Maybe someone takes a fall
Okay, business is business but why I gotta deal
With two-timing punks who think they know it all

Think they can play me, Like I wouldn't know
But if someone owes me I will always collect
But then I gotta smack — er-talk some sense into them
teach 'em some manners and teach 'em respect

(**TOFFEE** & **DR. MALAISE** *become the chorus, singing back up.*)

TONY	CHORUS
	Give the man respect
Is that too much to ask?	
	Just show the man respect
You know I'm asking you nice	
	He's asking for respect
I earned it	
	All he wants is respect
I won't ask you twice	

At home, here's the thing, I'm supposed to be king
You know what I'm sayin' Like I'm the last word
But the wife, the complaining The kids, always "gimme"
I'm lucky some days If I can make myself heard

Now I love my kids And I love my wife too
And I don't mean to sound like an unfeeling louse
But I'm the provider here, I'm Mr. Money
I oughtta be king of the hill in my house

And don't get me started on my mommy dearest
Who thinks that I live just to put her away
She's made my dead father into some kind of saint
Which he ain't, But we'll save that for some other day

So now I'm the bad son, Or stupid, or worse
I'm the one who would lock her up, Throw out the key
It's tempting, but mostly I just want to slap her
And yell "Shut up, Ma, show some respect to me"

TONY	CHORUS
	Give the man respect
I don't get no respect	
	Just show the man respect
Everyone is always in my face	
	He's asking for respect
It's the least I deserve	
	You give the man respect
You should all know your place	
	Give the man respect

My living conditions are very stressful
                         Just show the man respect
Makes me want to break a leg or two
                         He's askin' for respect
Blow some people away, y'know
                         Just give it to him
What else can I do?
I need respect   R-E-S-P-E-C-T
Respect!   Respect!

(*Lights return to normal.*)

MALAISE. I just don't remember you being that hip about it. More Perry Como.

TONY. But I'm changed now, Doc. Maybe it was you, or all this Prozac –

(*He pops a pill.*)

TONY. You're sure this crap ain't addictive?

MALAISE. Tony, I think what you're doing, putting your family and friends through all this grief –

TONY. As if they don't put me through grief? Why do you think I had to come to you in the first place? It ain't easy being in the kind of position I'm in. What with that FBI Agent breathin down my neck, fillin my wife's head full of these witness protection fairytales! You gotta do this for me. You were the one that said I needed to act on my suppressed thoughts.

MALAISE. Tony, faking your own death and then disguising yourself as a mourning woman to sneak into you own wake is hardly a suppressed thought. Its – Its – I'm not sure what it is. I'll have to look it up in the annals of psychology.

TONY. You stop being anal. – you're a psychologist not a proctologist. Necessary, Doc, is what this is, if I'm gonna find out who's been trying to take me down.

MALAISE. Well, you should at least tell your wife.

TONY. Forget about it! She and that priest of hers – I won't be surprised if one of them done it.

MALAISE. (*Realization*) Maybe this is a good thing. You're opening up, letting out some of your suppressed doubts.

TONY. I'm gonna be opening a few heads when I find out who it was that tried suppressin me with a car bomb.

MALAISE. (*Nervously changing subject*) I think we can use this to get beneath some more grave issues.

TONY. And I'm gonna issue some to beneath the grave.

MALAISE. Tony, the roots of your depression – these are the things you should be concentrating on. Your doubts about your wife and your mother –

TONY. Hey – don't even go there! You leave my crazy mother out of this. And as far as my wife – if she found out I was still alive, she'd wanta know who the crispy critter was that got toasted in my car when the bomb went off.

MALAISE. Who was it?

TONY. One of the girls from the club who was borrowing the car. She turned on the ignition – Badda Bang – badda BOOM!

MALAISE. Borrowing the car? I thought it blew up in a motel parking lot at 3:00 AM?

TONY. Well, yeah. She was borrowing it to go fetch us something from the all night liquor store.

(*He winks and starts to walk to a woman at a near by table.*)

TONY. You know, after you're dead – you feel so alive! I guess its that revenge thing that gets the blood flowing and the electrons in the brain clickin and all.

MALAISE. (*Pulling* **TONY** *away*) Tony, I think I may have some extra strength Prozac in my purse.

(*She begins to dig into her purse.*)

TONY. Hey – Doc. I've gone along with you plenty. Now its time you go along with me here. I ain't gonna run no more. I'm gonna face this demon head on, tonight. That's what you've been tellin me to do all this time

– face my demons. Well, tonight I'm willing to stand up to them and have it out. Are you with me?

MALAISE. Of course I'm with you, Tony. But –

TONY. Okay, I won't keep up the charade much longer. I hate wearing these strippers clothes anyway. This thong is killing me. I just want to pick the right time, yea know? It'll be interesting to see everyone's reaction, won't it?

MALAISE. I won't miss it for the world.

(**FATHER** *approaches,* **TONY** *hides his face under the veil again.*)

FATHER. Are you friends of the family?

MALAISE. Yes, I was Tony's doc –

(**TONY** *jabs her*)

MALAISE. – (*Putting on low class accent*) Dock union representative. (*Trying to act tough*) You know, long shore men – corrupt union – that sort of thing?

FATHER. I'm not sure I –

MALAISE. And this is Tony's cousin, Antoinette. She danced at one of his clubs.

FATHER. Oh – I'm not sure I've ever been to one of his clubs.

MALAISE. Oh, you'd know if you had been there. Badda Bangs – that's the name. Its a strip club. Right over here are some of the other dancers that came to pay their respects. (*She goes to a table with several women*). But Antoinette will be happy to make the introductions – as they're all her compatriots.

TONY. (*In high voice*) Yes, well, this is Double Jointed Donna, and this is Triple Jointed Tina, and this is Naughty Nina and this is (*picking a man*) – ah – Buffy. We'll all be dancing in black all week.

MALAISE. The dance of the seven vales.

TONY. Yeah, they'll be seven dancers on at a time.

FATHER. I see – well, I really won't see.

MALAISE. No, I suppose you wouldn't would you, Father.

TONY. Were you going to start the ceremony?

FATHER. Oh, well – yes, I suppose I should. I better check with the widow first. If you'll excuse me?

(*He leaves.* **TONY** *lifts vale.*)

TONY. Check out the widow is more like it. And what's this seven vales crap? We ain't got a single doll named veil dancing at the club!

MALAISE. The dance of the seven vales was the first striptease, from biblical times.

TONY. You mean stripping is catholic?

MALAISE. Forget about it.

TONY. (*The Italian way*) Forget about it!

MALAISE. What?

TONY. You can't just say, forget about it – otherwise it doesn't transfer your true intention. To correctly communicate your inner meaning of your feelings, you have to over dramatically emphasize in a stereotypical ethnic fashion. You can't just say, "Forget about it." You have to say (*Italian way*) "Forget about it!"

MALAISE. Forget about it.

TONY. Closer, but not quite –

MALAISE. No, I mean it – forget about it.

TONY. Try it with more ethnicity. "Forget about it!"

MALAISE. Forget –

TONY. No – "Forget – "

(**TONY** *continues to try and teach* **MALAISE** *how to say "Forget about it," while she is trying to tell him to just forget about teaching her. Lights fade. Music. All characters mingle.*)

1st Break Mingles

CHRIS – *mingles with a cell phone – making Hollywood deals, casting his story which he lets everyone know he's sold to HBO. He'll even offer auditions to women in the audience. He must find someone from the audience who is large and willing to play Big Kitty.*

TOFFEE – *mingles, asking people how long a woman should wait after her husbands death to start a new relationship. She asks people if they think Priests ever leave their vocation for the love of the right woman. "There's something so exciting about forbidden fruit."*

TONY – *mingles as Antoinette in his dress, talking in a false high voice. He asks woman if they'd like to audition for Badda-Bangs – he knows the owners and can get them a job there. He asks people how they know Tony and the Alto family. He asks if they know anyone who may not have liked Tony.*

UNCLE SENIOR – *mingles, letting everyone know that he's running things now – that he's the boss like he always should have been. He points out Tony as an example of what happens if you don't follow the old ways.*

NONA – *mingles, alternating between crying for her Tony and cursing him for trying to send her away. She warns people that they shouldn't be too quick to try and get rid of the old folks. You never know when they might strike back.*

FATHER – *mingles, asking guests if they have any idea how to start a funeral. He's never done one before. They're sort of like weddings, only more negative, right?*

DR. MALAISE – *mingles, giving people quick psycho-analysis with ink blot tests and prescribing long vacations, donating their savings to worthy causes, stress reduction through ballet lessons, getting in touch with their inner child by going back to pre-school, avoiding sexual frustration by joining the religious cult – the Moonies or Hassedics.*

Scene II

(*Theme music. Lights fade out, then up.* **FATHER** *is by the urn, his service book open. Everyone is present.*)

FATHER. Dearly beloved. We are gathered here today to join with our friends in celebrating this most special of occasions.

(*Everyone looks at one another, puzzled.*)

TOFFEE. Psssst! Father, I think you may be on the wrong page.

FATHER. Oh (*turns pages*) ah – yes, lets see. (*Finds his place, clears throat and begins his sermon*) Anthony Alto – Tony to his friends. What can we say about Tony Alto that hasn't already been said – under deposition? (*Sermonizing*) He was many things to many people – husband, father, friend, godfather, goodfella, wise guy, soprano in the choir – a man who knew law and order but sometimes had the NYPD Blues. Tony Alto was a take charge kind of guy. Whatever he felt needed to be done, he would go the whole nine yards. In his own favorite expression – Badda Bing, Badda Who.

CHRIS. Boom!

FATHER. Yes, boom is what happened to our Tony. And now, here he lies (*pointing to urn*) – er – well at least what's left of him – ah – (*looks back in book*) And now, here before Gods eyes and those of many friends and relatives, we have come to honor one of our most holy of sacraments. For today, we share in the happiness of a new beginning – in the paving of a new road – in a journey of two hearts –

CHRIS. I think yous are on the wrong page again there Father.

UNCLE SENIOR. But not far off. Huh, Nona?

NONA. Bite your tongue and choke on it.

UNCLE SENIOR. What's with you?

NONA. What's with me? What's with me? My own flesh and blood is dead! Isn't that enough?

(*Sob*) He may have been a no good, back-stabbing, disrespectful, house thief – but he was still my son. *My son!* (*Cry*)

TONY. (*To* **MALAISE**) You see, I told you she loved me.

NONA. You? I don't love you, for Christ sake.

TONY. (*Taking off vale*) It's me, ma!

NONA. Who are you calling ma? I'm not your mother. I don't have no pillar of salt ugly daughter.

TONY. I'm not your daughter, ma. I'm your son.

NONA. I don't have no transvestite son neither. That's my son (*pointing to urn*) My one and only son Tony. (*Sob*)

TONY. I'm Tony, Ma.

FATHER. You're not Tony. You're his cousin, Antoinette – the stripper.

TOFFEE. He ain't got no cousin Antoinette. Although he's gotten plenty of strippers.

NONA. Antoinette?

(**TONY** *starts taking off the shawl & dress. He has his clothes on underneath.*)

FATHER. Young lady, I know that may be your profession, but you can't do that here.

CHRIS. I'll say, you're too ugly to do it anywhere there's lights on and guys are sober.

TONY. I ain't no stripper. I'm freakin Tony Alto.

(*He takes off the hat and vale.*)

EVERYONE (*Except* **MALAISE**) TONY?

(**NONA** *clutches her heart and faints into a table of guests.* **TONY** *dashes to her.*)

TONY. Ma?

(*He lifts her up. She opens her eyes – hits him and pushes him away.*)

NONA. Get away from me you, you – you – You're trying to give me a heart attack? I wouldn't let you put me away in a home, so now you're trying to kill my heart!

(*Pounds her chest*) Here, here take it – rip it out with your bare hands.

TONY. That would take a steak and a silver bullet.

NONA. We're having steak?

UNCLE SENIOR. You ain't dead?

FATHER. You're not dead?

CHRIS. (*to guest*) He's not dead?

NONA. (*Slaps a guest on the shoulder*) You told me he was dead!

TOFFEE. You're not dead?

TONY. Do I look freakin dead to you?

TOFFEE. No – but in second you will be – you –

(*She starts beating him.*)

How could you do such a thing to your own family? What you put me and the kids through! You crazy freaking SOB!

TONY. Stop it Toffee, stop it. I'm sorry, for Christ sake.

(*He holds her off. She stops hitting him.*)

TOFFEE. (*to* **MALAISE**) I wonder what a shrink would say about this kind of behavior, huh?

MALAISE. Well – I – (*She catches herself and stops*)

CHRIS. Shrink? (*Laugh*) Who needs a freakin shrink? Wise-guys like Tony, they don't need no fruit of the loom head doctor. Right Tony?

TONY. (*uneasy*) Yeah, right.

CHRIS. Besides, if he did go to some head shrinker, after he got better we'd have to ice the doc cause the shrink would know too much. Right Tony?

(**MALAISE** *looks at* **TONY.**)

TONY. I ain't going to no freakin head doctor, okay?

FATHER. I'm confused. If you're alive –

TONY. Surprised ain't yea?

FATHER. Well, yes of course, but –

TONY. Freakin disappointed is what you are!

TOFFEE. What? Father Flip is here for us, Tony.

TONY. He's here for you alright.

TOFFEE. And what the hell is that supposed to mean?

TONY. Oh, you know what it means.

TOFFEE. (*Mad*) Well then you remind me!

FATHER. Might I interject with a question?

TONY. You can freakin interject all you what, Father. That's what you're really good at.

FATHER. Thank you – I think. Well, if you are alive – then who, might I ask, is in the urn?

CHRIS. Hey, that's one good freakin interjection there father. I mean, lets face it, Tony, when your SUV blew we thought it was either a hit or your firestone tires. Either way, who ever was inside got a little past done in the deep fat fryer, if you know what I mean. Naturally we though it was you, being your car and all. (*To guest*) I mean, that's what he told me.

TONY. Was he there?

CHRIS. That's a good question. Was you there?

(*Who knows what they'll say , probably "no."*)

TOFFEE. Tony, you're avoiding the question.

TONY. Which question?

NONA. You know which question. Who was in your car?

TONY. One of the girls.

TOFFEE. One of the girls? One of your goom madahs, you mean? One of your strippers!

CHRIS. Exotic dancers.

TOFFEE. Exotic my googootz.

TONY. She was borrowing the freakin car.

UNCLE SENIOR. At two in the morning, in the Miller's Crossing Motel parking lot?

CHRIS. I though you was doing some freakin business?

TOFFEE. Oh, he was doing some business alright. He was doing that dancer. (*To* **TONY**) You strunz!

(*She hits* **TONY**.)

TONY. Hey, hey – hey! Where else am I gonna go when you're with your goom badah priest here?

FATHER. I'm not sure I like the sound of that.

TOFFEE. (*Offended*) My what?

TONY. Don't you freakin go and try and play innocent with me. You think I'm stewnoda?

NONA. Tony – he's a man of the cloth.

TONY. Yeah, the loin cloth.

FATHER. Mr. Alto? I'm – – I assure you – – This isn't some-thing out of some pulp fiction novel – (*starting to leave*) Perhaps I better inform the hearse there's no need for him.

TONY. There still might be, father.

UNCLE SENIOR. And maybe sooner than you'd think.

(**FATHER** *exits fast.*)

TOFFEE. This is ridiculous! (*Exiting*) I'm getting some fresh air.

TONY. Going to confess to your priest?

(*She gives him a mean gesture and exits.*)

NONA. (*to a man in the audience*) I thought this would be a nice quiet mourning. Just a little wake, with a few deep sobs and heart felt moans. But nooooo. Not the Altos. Not my family. They refuse to let the dead rest. They gotta drag'em back up and have them kick you in the gut. This is killing me. They got no respect for their elders, these kids now a days. No respect. I need a seat. Get up and give an old lady your seat!

(*She forces the man to stand up.*)

UNCLE SENIOR. That's right – no respect. So, Tony, if you wasn't in the car when it took to the sky, why'd you let your family and friends think you was dead? You scared, Tony? Is that it? The top guy Tony Alto is run-ning scared? Maybe you've gone and lost your nerve? Maybe you shoulda never been tryin to run things in the first place? (*Approaching the standing man*) Look at him. Look at the big Tony Alto, sneaking into his own wake dressed as a woman. Now, doesn't that sound like he's scared?

(*Who knows what they'll say.*)

TONY. Hey, I had my reasons, uncle Senior.

CHRIS. (*to the standing man*) Yeah – he had is reasons.

UNCLE SENIOR. (*to* **CHRIS**) Like what?

CHRIS. Well, – Well – er – ah –

(**CHRIS** *tries to think of a reason. He turns to an audience member.*)

CHRIS. Go on, you tells uncle Senior Tony's reason for laying low.

(*Who knows what they'll say – hopefully that he wanted to find out who was trying to kill him.*)

CHRIS. Yeah – like she said. But Uncle Senior, you seem to be looking more upset once you found out Tony was alive than when yous thought he was dead.

UNCLE SENIOR. What are you talking about? You're patza! I came to his wake didn't I? I brought my only sister, to give her strength and support in her hour of need.

NONA. Bite your tongue and choke on it!

UNCLE SENIOR. What? What's wrong with you Nona?

NONA. (*Standing up*) What's wrong with me? (*To guest*) What's wrong with you? You plannin on standing all night? You're giving me agida standing around like that, hovering over me. Sit down. And he wants to know what's wrong with me? (*To* **UNCLE SENIOR**) I'm getting older. It's what's wrong with everybody. You'll see. It'll start getting to you too. There's no escaping it. You start life with "always" and end up with "Depends." From the moment we're born, we start to die.

CHRIS. But some people try to hurry things up, don't they, uncle Senior?

UNCLE SENIOR. What are you talking about?

CHRIS. I'm talking about what we do.

UNCLE SENIOR. I don't know nothin about what you do.

CHRIS. Yous just saying that cause you're afraid there's a wire here some wheres. Being under indictdidlement and all as you are, you gotta be freakin careful.

UNCLE SENIOR. They ain't got nothin they can stick to me. Nothin, unless someone in the family was to sell out and take some witness relocation crap. Someone who couldn't take it anymore and never should have been taking it in the first place.

CHRIS. Someone like Tony? Is that what you're saying uncle Senior?

UNCLE SENIOR. I'm not sayin nothin.

CHRIS. Yeah – well that's just the way it should be too. As a matter of fact, Big Kitty and I was just saying nothin the other day – (*To man pre-selected to be Big Kitty*) Weren't we, Big Kitten? Come here a moment, will ya?

(**CHRIS** *gets "Big Kitty" up and together they approach* **UNCLE SENIOR.**)

CHRIS. Yeah, Big Kitty here and I was just saying nothin about loyalty. You know how yous is always talking about respect? Well, we was talking about loyalty. Weren't we, Big Kitty?

(*Who knows what he'll say. Probably "yeah."*)

CHRIS. Yeah. He's very soft spoken, Big Kitty. But he ain't no kitten when push comes to shove if you know what I mean. Badda Bang, Badda Boom – right Big Kitty?

(*He'll say right.*)

CHRIS. Freakin right alright! (*To Big Kitty*) Oh (*handing Kitty a gun*) You left this in my car, Big Kitty. I know it has sentimental value to yous. (*To* **SENIOR**) Anyways, Big Kitty here and I was not talking about loyalty and what to do when someone ain't being straight with it, you know what I mean.

UNCLE SENIOR. You better be careful what you're saying, Chris. Don't be a shiddrull.

(*The* **DELIVERY MAN** (*same actor as Father*) *enters with a box of flowers.*)

DELIVERY MAN. Is this the Tony Alto wake?

UNCLE SENIOR. Yeah – its supposed to be.

TONY. (*to* **MALAISE**) Look, how nice! Someone remembered me.

(*Suddenly, everyone moves in slow motion as the delivery man opens the box and pulls a gun, turning it on* **TONY**. *Everyone screams in slow motion and begins to hide behind audience members as he shoots twice, missing once and hitting* **TONY** *in the arm the second time.*)

TONY. Slow motion stinks.

(**TONY** *grabs the gun, they struggle turning it at audience members. Once* **TONY** *gets the gun away from the assassin –*)

CHRIS. (*to Big Kitty*) Let him have it, Big Kitty!

(*The audience member will shoot –* **CHRIS** *keeps him shooting until* **TOFFEE** *dashes in, hearing the shots.* **CHRIS** *has him stop so* **TOFFEE** *can cross, then finish shooting the gun at the assassin*)

CHRIS. Nice shootin there, Big Kitty. I mean, you got him the first time so you didn't really have to keep pluggin away like that. After all, bullets are expensive. (*Taking gun*) I'll ditch the piece, while yous have a seat.

(**CHRIS** *re-seats audience member as* **TOFFEE** *goes to look at* **TONY**'s *arm.*)

TOFFEE. So, is this gonna be your funeral or isn't?

TONY. I don't know – you tell me? (*To* **DELIVERY MAN**) Or should I say (*grabs him by the chest, slams him against wall*) You tell me!

DELIVERY MAN. (*In pain*) Chest Hair!

TONY. Come on, fellah – Before you die – tell me who put you up to this – Come clean.

(*Music begins for "**COME CLEAN**"*)

TOFFEE.

YOUR DAYS ARE NUMBERED
YOU'VE BEEN SHOT THROUGH THE HEART
YOU WANNA BARE YOUR SOUL
BEFORE YOU DEPART?
WE CAN DO THIS THE HARD WAY
YOU KNOW WHAT I MEAN
OR YOU CAN COME CLEAN

CHORUS.

COME CLEAN

DELIVERY MAN. You're right, I –

TOFFEE.

SO WHY CLAM UP
AND TAKE THE SECRET TO YOUR GRAVE
FINGER THE FINK
THINK OF THE TROUBLE YOU'LL SAVE
DON'T HOLD OUT ON US, MISTER
SPILL THE BEANS
FELLAH, COME CLEAN

DELIVERY MAN. Okay, I'll tell you. It –

CHORUS.

COME CLEAN WHILE YOU CAN
AND TAKE A LOAD OFF YOUR CHEST

TONY.

YOU CLUE US IN
AND WE'LL TAKE CARE OF THE REST

CHORUS.

COME CLEAN AND YOUR CONSCIENCE
WILL FINALLY BE FREE

TOFFEE.

SPEAK YOUR PEACE
CLEAR THE AIR
YOU CAN SHARE IT WITH ME
COME CLEAN

DELIVERY MAN. I'm trying to tell you it was –

NONA.

> JUST BLOW THE WHISTLE
> DROP A DIME ON THE GUY
> WE'LL GO INVESTIGATE
> AS SOON AS YOU DIE
> YOU CAN RAT ON THE LOUSE
> TELL US ALL WHAT YOU SEEN
> YOU CAN COME CLEAN

CHORUS.

> COME CLEAN

DELIVERY MAN. Alright, I –

UNCLE SENIOR.

> SO PUT US WISE
> AND YOU CAN SING LIKE A BIRD
> YOU WANNA SOUND OFF
> WE'LL MAKE SURE THAT YOU'RE HEARD
> SPIT IT OUT
> COUGH IT UP
> SPILL YOUR GUTS

CHRIS.

> – OR YOUR SPLEEN

CHORUS.

> COME ON, COME CLEAN

DELIVERY MAN. You're not making this easy –

CHORUS.

> COME CLEAN
> YOU CAN LET THE CAT OUT OF THE BAG

TOFFEE.

> WHY NOT CONFESS
> BEFORE YOUR TOE WEARS A TAG
> WHO'RE YOU PROTECTING
> TELL US
> WHAT DOES IT MEAN
>
> YOU GOTTA FESS UP

CHRIS.

> UNLOAD

NONA.

TIP YOUR HAND

UNCLE SENIOR.

BLOW THE GAFF

TONY.

DISH THE DIRT

DELIVERY MAN. Will you all shut up?

ALL.

COME CLEAN

(*He dies.*)

CHRIS. Maybe we shouldn't have sung that last verse?

(*Lights out. Body is removed in black out. Characters mingle until everyone is served entree. Cast takes a break.*)

Scene III

(Music. Lights dim and come up full. **MALAISE** *is bandaging* **TONY***'s arm while* **TOFFEE** *holds it still. Everyone but father is near by.)*

TONY. I know this ain't your usual doctoring, so thanks Doc. At least I didn't get no scarface.

MALAISE. Tony, after meeting all these people you've talked about in our sessions, I think I have a better outlook on the external forces in your life.

TOFFEE. The worse external forces are the ones made of lead.

MALAISE. I wouldn't want to make any snap judgements and possibly misrepresent anyone –

TOFFEE. Go right a head. TV and movies, they misrepresent us Italian-Americans all the time.

TONY. Hey, Once upon a time in America – things were even worse for us.

TOFFEE. That was the jews.

TONY. Jews, Italians – same thing, only we got better food.

TOFFEE. Don't worry about offending nobody here, Doctor Malaise. You just tells us what you think.

MALAISE. Well, its not really what I think that matters. Its what Tony thinks, about the people surrounding him.

TONY. I think someone's trying to kill me, that's what I think. And don't go tellin me that's some paranoia crap or nothin.

MALAISE. No, I wouldn't consider bullets to be a dementia of paranoia.

TOFFEE. Its gettin worse and worse – and Tony won't even consider the witness relocation deal – like his friend Mickey Blue Eyes took.

(She walks to a man in the audience.)

TOFFEE. And look, he was nice enough to come out of hiding to attend your funeral. (*Sits on his lap*) God, it was so nice of you to show up like this, knowing that there's a contact out on your life and all. I mean, it really meant a lot to me and Tony.

(*She kisses him on both cheeks as* **CHRIS** *walks up.*)

CHRIS. Mickey? It's freakin amazing! I never would have recognoitered you or nothin, what with all that plastical sturgery and all. Look, his eyes ain't even blue no more. Mickey, pal, come with me a moment I need to shows you somethin out front.

(*As* **CHRIS** *takes him out.*)

TONY. (*to* **TOFFEE**) How'd you recognize that was Mickey Blue Eyes even after he changed his look and all?

TOFFEE. When a gal sits on a guys lap, it ain't the face she's recognizing.

(*There is the sound of gunshots outside.*)

TOFFEE. (*To date of man taken out*) I hope you have a ride home tonight.

(**CHRIS** *enters, putting his gun away.*)

CHRIS. I freakin love closing contracts.

MALAISE. (*turning away from* **CHRIS**) Oh God – I didn't just see that!

CHRIS. See what – me just make 50 grand?

UNCLE SENIOR. (*to* **CHRIS**) You gavone!

CHRIS. What?

UNCLE SENIOR. Clean it up! You think the father here is gonna pick up after you?

CHRIS. Oh, yeah, right (*starts to leave, stops at door*) But where do I dump him?

UNCLE SENIOR. Just across the back alley there's a restaurant called Hannabal's.

CHRIS. Right.

(*He exits.*)

MALAISE. I can't be hearing this.

UNCLE SENIOR. You ain't heard nothin and you ain't seen nothin. So forget about it.

(**CHRIS** *enters with audience member in sunglasses and Fedor.*)

CHRIS. Hey, look, it's Mickey's twin cousin, Mikey. He's just a little late for the wake.

TOFFEE. (*Showing him to his seat*) Here's a seat open and hey (*motioning to his date*) Maybe you can lucky tonight. (*Winks*)

CHRIS *exits.*

TOFFEE. Tony you should have taken that deal last year when they first offered it to you. Same as Mickey.

TONY. And look at where he is now – entree at Hannabals – Stata zete about that already!

TOFFEE. Stata Zete yourself. (*To* **MALAISE**) What kind of a father is he to his family? I can't take this no more. (*To* **TONY**) Living with you is like – is like living in a casino. Sometimes you win, but you always know you're gonna lose big – and soon. It's killing me. Its killing our family. Sometimes I think maybe we'd be better off if you *was* dead.

TONY. (*to* **MALAISE**) You see – you see? This is what I have to put up with.

MALAISE. But this is good. This is open. Its getting it all out there.

TONY. Getting it all out there? Getting it all out there never helped anyone other than strippers and people with food poisonin.

MALAISE. Tony – I realize you may not have that much faith in modern psychology, but there are plenty of examples of success. Why, just look at this woman over here – (*She goes to a female guest*). In the past ten years alone she has had 15 husbands – 15! Once we probed deep into her subconscious history, we discovered that as a child she lived in a small apartment and was never allowed to collect anything. She's obviously gone a little over board making up for it – but at least now we can start her on the road to recovery. Why, she's already divorced four of them. (*To woman, motioning to* *her date*) And don't marry this one.

(*She walks to another "patient."*)

MALAISE. And take this man over here. Whenever he heard the name of a certain German sausage spoken out loud, he would jump down onto all fours, howl like a dog and furiously chase anything that moved, biting it severely. Ankles were never safe within eye sight of him until we discovered that as a small child he had an aggressive relationship with a dachshund with a nasty disposition that lived next door. Now that we've begun the treatments, he no longer needs the flee collar.

(*She hands him a dog biscuit and pats him on the head.*)

MALAISE. Sit boy – sit. That's a good boy. So, now, Toffee, what did you mean by sometimes you think you'd be better off if Tony really were dead?

TONY. Yeah?

MALAISE. And Tony, you have to be nonjudgmental about this. Just let your wife express herself without fear of incrimination.

TOFFEE. That's the thing all the time – the fear. I wanted to be married to Tony Alto. Instead, I got married to the mob. We're not close no more. Things have changed and I ain't sure they're for the better.

TONY. What do you mean? I got you a huge house, a new car, a George Forman Grill –

MALAISE. Tony! Button it! (*To* TOFFEE) So, what is missing that used to be there? The trust? The intimacy?

TOFFEE. (*Realization*) Yeah, yeah – especially the intimacy and the trust. I pretend to look the other way at his fooling around. But I ain't fooling myself.

MALAISE. So some times you wonder if there's some way that could all be changed? If there was some way to start a new life?

TOFFEE. Who wouldn't? But you can't divorce the mob – no wonder we're all catholic huh?

MALAISE. So that is why you said sometimes you wish Tony were dead. Because then you'd be free of the mob – free to find someone you can trust, find some intimacy with?

TOFFEE. (*almost ashamed*) Yeah.

TONY. And collect on my million dollar life insurance.

(*She glares at him.*)

MALAISE. Which explains your abnormally close relationship with your priest.

TOFFEE. What?

TONY. Oh – now we're getting somewhere. Don't stop now Doc.

MALAISE. Father Flip is obviously someone you feel you can trust, and since he is filling one of your needs – trust, you naturally look to him to fill your other major need – intimacy.

TOFFEE. Are you crazy? He's a freakin priest!

MALAISE. Priests have broken their vows before. Some women even find the challenge to be more enticing, an attraction. The same way certain women are attracted to (*she goes to a man in the audience and runs her hands over his shoulders*) bad boys. (*She pulls herself away and continues*) Its obvious that you are attracted to the unobtainable Father Flip, just as you were attracted to the bad boy Tony Alto.

(**FATHER** *enters and approaches them.* **TOFFEE** *gets very nervous.*)

TOFFEE. Well – I ain't your patient, Doctor Malaise. Keep your head shrinkin to my pig headed husband. I need a drink.

(*She quickly exits to bar.*)

TONY. You're on a roll now, Doc. Why don't you try the Father?

FATHER. (*Smiling, thinking sex*) Try me how?

MALAISE. Just a figure of speech Father.

(*He looks disappointed. She approaches him.*)

MALAISE. You seem to be a man who's not quite comfortable with his station in life. Not quite confident – sometimes even nervous for apparently no reason – as if you're afraid of being discovered.

TONY. Oh – she's got you there Father, ain't she?

FATHER. Well – I – er – I don't know what you mean.

MALAISE. From listening to your ceremony, I would guess that you haven't been in the priest hood long, Father.

(**CHRIS** *re-enters.*)

FATHER. Well, no, not too long. I'll be celebrating the anniversary of answering the call next month. It will be two years.

CHRIS. That's a long time to hold it in.

FATHER. No, my son. That's how long I've been in the priesthood.

CHRIS. You mean how long you've been out of prison.

(*They all look at* **CHRIS**.)

CHRIS. Tony asked that I do some checking up on you, father. You was in the big house there for a few years. You was part of Donnie Brasco's gang. Nabbed you for being the driver on a hit. Accessary. And the hit was on one of ours.

FATHER. I was lost, but found my way behind bars.

CHRIS. Found your way to an early release by becoming a priest. (*To* **TONY**) This guys a freakin smart one, he is. And Brasco's been looking to muscle in on our territory. (*To* **FATHER**) I bet you're still friendly with some of your old pals, ain't yeah?

FATHER. I'm a purveyor of the good book, now

CHRIS. From what I hear you was preying on the good Brook – she being the Warden's college age daughter. (*To* **TONY** & **MALAISE**) While in the slammer he was using his priesthood schoolin scam as a ways to get to the prison chapel and give that co-ed a few religious experiences.

FATHER. Alright – alright. It's true. It's all true. (*Looking up to heaven*) I've tried. Oh dear Lord, I've really tried. I know you've been calling me – and God, you know I've tried to answer – but I have call waiting and the line is always getting interrupted. I don't mean to be putting you on hold, but –

(**TOFFEE** *approaches with her drink. He throws himself at her.*)

FATHER. Toffee Alto – when we thought your husband was finally dead, I bought you this –

(*He hands her a ring box.*)

TOFFEE. Father Flip?

FATHER. Your husband's probably gonna have me wasted before the night is through, so I just wanted you to have this – as something to remember me by. (*To* **CHRIS**) Alright, whenever you're ready. I'll be waiting outside – giving myself last rights.

(**FATHER** *exits.*)

TOFFEE. You touch that good man, Chris and I'll cut your chip pollas off!

(**MALAISE** *puts her hand out.* **TOFFEE** *looks at her, then at* **TONY**. *She gives* **MALAISE** *the ring box, without opening it.*)

TOFFEE. He's a good man. (*To* **TONY**) Nothing ever really happened. (*To* **CHRIS**) And you, you're a – I can't say it in polite company.

CHRIS. I'm a loyal guy. (*Puts his arm around* **TONY**) Tony's gonna make me a made man.

TOFFEE. Loyal? You? (*To* **TONY**) He's sold his story to TV

CHRIS. It's not TV – its HBO.

(**TONY** *glares at him.* **CHRIS** *quickly removes his arm and moves away from* **TONY** *– scared.*)

TOFFEE. 'Claims they're gonna make it into some kind of series. His producer's sittin right over there – (*points to audience member*) with the strippers from Badda Bangs.

CHRIS. They ain't strippers – they's expiring actresses.

TONY. (*Approaching* **CHRIS**) What? You can't do that! I told you! (*Grabs him by the lapels and pins him up against the wall*) I forbid you!

TOFFEE. There's your loyalty, Tony. He wants to die in a mansion in Beverly Hills, not in a land fill in New Jersey.

CHRIS. I thought you was dead, Tony!

UNCLE SENIOR. Half a million they promised him

(**TONY** *slaps* **CHRIS** *across the face.*)

UNCLE SENIOR. – that's the word on the street. Half a mill –

(**TONY** *slaps* **CHRIS** *across the face the other way.*)

UNCLE SENIOR. – to sell out his family and friends.

(**TONY** *slaps* **CHRIS** *upside the head.*)

CHRIS. I wasn't freakin sellin nobody out!

(**TONY** *continues to slap around* **CHRIS** *during* **UNCLE SENIORS***'s speech – almost in a three stooges manner.*)

UNCLE SENIOR. Kept asking to be a made man! But Tony never made you one – the only thing he ever done right. You knew he'd never make a strunz like you a made guy. So you decided to sell us out – sell us all out. You started making that deal months ago and you knew if Tony ever found out, you'd be in that land fill faster than a tourist running from The Mexican water fountain.

CHRIS. Hey, hey – (*pointing to man in audience*) he came to me! We was just talkin. Nothin wrong with talkin. (*To* **TONY**) Tony, honest, I'd never cross yous. I'm your man. I'm –

(**TONY** *punches* **CHRIS**, *knocking him to the floor. He picks* **CHRIS** *up again.*)

CHRIS. Why didn't you hit him (*pointing to same man*)? He's the producer!

TONY. I would, but (*looking at man*) it looks like he's been hit enough already. (*Motioning to the guys date*) Probably by her. (*Turns back to* **MALAISE**) And what about uncle Senior, Doc?

UNCLE SENIOR. What about me? What do you mean what about me? I'm under indictment, for Christ sake. They got me wearing these collars and bracelets and anklets – (*To* **MALAISE**) You're his doctor, right? Tell him he's being paranoid. You've seen it in him.

MALAISE. I thought I was seeing it in him – until I met you. Then I realized this wasn't just a phobia or a projection. You are obviously suffering from a Little Caesar complex – a feeling of being passed over and forgotten – a feeling of lost entitlement. These feelings manifest themselves as resentment towards your nephew. A resentment with potentially dangerous repercussions.

UNCLE SENIOR. Does anyone know what the hell this lady's talking about?

NONA. She's saying you want my son dead – that's what she's saying. My own brother!

UNCLE SENIOR. You want to analyze something? Well analyze this (*points to* **NONA**)!

NONA. What? Me? What's there to analyze? I'm just an old woman.

MALAISE. And probably the root of Tony's deepest anxieties.

TONY. Hey, hey – I told you doc, you don't go there.

NONA. Go where? I don't see us going anywhere. Are we supposed to be going somewhere?

MALAISE. Tony, your mother is obviously suffering from the onset of senility and possibly Alzheimer.

NONA. (*Scratching her leg*) Is that what it is? I thought is was just a rash.

MALAISE. Tony, your mother –

TONY. I don't want to hear this!

TOFFEE. Don't want to hear what? What everyone else in

this family has know for a long time – That you moth-
ers' off her rocker?

NONA. Of course I'm off my rocker. My rocker's at home, its
not here at the funeral. Why would I bring my rocker
to a funeral? (*To* **TOFFEE**) Who are you anyway?

TOFFEE. I'm Toffee – your daughter in law, remember Ma?

NONA. Were you at my son's wedding?

TOFFEE. Yeah. I was the one in white!

NONA. I thought that's where we met. (*To audience*) There
were a lot of people at Tony's wedding.

MALAISE. Tony, your resistance to explore your relationship
with your mother is natural – you're feeling guilt over
knowing she needs to be placed in a nursing home
and fearing her wrath if you actually do it.

NONA. He should fear more than that! I gave birth to that
son-of-a-bitch, I can take it away too. One phone call.
One phone call's all it takes. I got the number written
down by my phone too. You try and put me away in a
home, and by God I'm gonna call that number. Or did
I call –

TONY. Ma, you don't know what you're saying!

MALAISE. That's right Tony. She doesn't know what she's
saying – or what she's doing or even done. Her survival
instincts have over taken her motherly instincts and
in her volatile mental state she is capable of virtually
anything.

UNCLE SENIOR. I'll say.

NONA. Bite your tongue and –

UNCLE SENIOR & NONA. Choke on it!

TONY. If she did do somethin its because you put her up to
it, Uncle Senior. You was never good to me.

UNCLE SENIOR. I was never good to you? Ma-rown! I
deserve some honor – some Pritzi's honor! You – You
never show me no respect!

TONY. (*Angry*) Yeah, well that's because –

NONA. Ah, Shaddap you face!

MALAISE. Actually, Mrs. Alto – this is very therapeutic to –

NONA. Shaddap you face, too!

UNCLE SENIOR. You had that coming, you mitagan –

NONA. And Shaddap you face three!

MALAISE. Well, Tony, I think we've gone about as far as we can go in this session.

(*Another hitman dashes in with a long flower box*)

HITMAN. Tony Alto?

TONY. Yeah?

(*The* **HITMAN** *pulls a machine gun out of the box. He tries to shot, yelling "Die, Die, Die" but the gun jams.*)

HITMAN. Dam E-Bay! (*To* **TONY**) Sorry – can I get back to you later?

TONY. Sure.

HITMAN. Thanks.

(*As the hitman turns to leave,* **CHRIS**, **TONY**, **UNCLE SENIOR**, **NONA** *and* **TOFFEE** *pull guns and shot him. He staggers, falling out the door.* **CHRIS** *goes to the door.*)

CHRIS. (*Looks out*) Looks like the freezer at Hanabals is gonna be over stocked this week.

(**CHRIS** *exits.*)

TONY. That guy sure looked a lot like the last one – Wait – Now I recognize those guys! They're the Krays – hired triggers. Alright. I'm all confused here. So, I need you all to take a moment to fill out who you think has been trying to have me knocked off and why. Maybe you can help me in the serving of just desserts.

(*Black out.*)

3rd Break Mingle

TONY — *tells guests that he went to the hotel direct from the Doctors office, so whoever hired the Krays must have known he was seeing the Doc. He asks everyone their opinions.*

DR. MALAISE — *believes any one of them could have done it, as they are all highly emotional and therefore given to outbursts of extreme behavior. She offers everyone Prozac.*

CHRIS — *accuses Father Flip, he may still be a member of the Brasco gang and has the hots for Toffee. Didn't know Tony was seeing a shrink.*

FATHER — *accuses Toffee, she was fed up with Tony's infidelity and was too afraid to leave him. Didn't know Tony was seeing a shrink.*

TOFFEE — *accuses Nona, she's crazy, mean and vengeful. Knew Tony was seeing Dr. Malaise*

NONA — *accuses Uncle Senior, he hated her son — thought he should run things. Even gave her the number of the Krays and tried to talk her into calling them. Knew Tony was seeing a shrink, Tony let it slip once. She told Uncle Senior.*

UNCLE SENIOR — *accuses Chris, cause he was selling his story to HBO and Tony would have killed him. Knew Tony was seeing a shrink as Nona told him.*

Scene IV

(*Music. Lights dim, come up full. Everyone is present.*)

FATHER. Chris, if you wouldn't mind doing me a small favor?

CHRIS. Sure thing, Father. What is it?

FATHER. Don't let me know when its coming – and make it quick.

CHRIS. Whatever you want, Father. The customer always comes first.

TOFFEE. No one's gonna do a thing to you, Father. Not Chris, nor anyone else.

TONY. That would depend.

TOFFEE. (*Snapping*) On what?

TONY. On whether he was the one who put the hit on me. One of you here hired the Krays to take me down. And that's not something I take too kindly too.

MALAISE. (*Pulling out her note pad*) Of course you wouldn't, Tony. And it's good that you recognize that and voiced it. Now, would anyone in the group like to offer their comments – thoughts?

NONA. Yeah – How come creamed corn comes out the same way it goes in?

TONY. MA?

CHRIS. (*Shyly raising his hand*) I feel – I feel it was Father Flip.

MALAISE. (*Taking notes*) And why do you feel that, Chris?

CHRIS. He's got the Hots for Mrs. Alto.

NONA. (*Smiling fluttered*) Of course. I always was a considered a looker.

CHRIS. Mrs. Toffee Alto, that is. And he was a shooter for a rival family before he went into the slammer. So I'd say he had it two fold – his motive in others.

MALAISE. Very good. See how nice it feels to get it all off your chest?

CHRIS. Yeah – Yeah!

MALAISE. (*To* **FATHER**) Now, its your turn, Father. How do you feel about what Chris has just said?

FATHER. What? I feel he's wrong, is how I feel.

MALAISE. (*Writing*) You feel you've been misunderstood?

FATHER. Yes!

MALAISE. Well, tell the group *how* you feel you've been misunderstood.

FATHER. This – this is difficult.

MALAISE. Open up, Father. Share with the group.

FATHER. Well – alright. Yes, I have strong feelings for Toffee Alto. But they've been in response to her strong feelings for me. Her longing is so desperate, its entrapping.

MALAISE. (*writing*) Good word – go on.

FATHER. She wanted to be rid of her old life, of her cheating and neglectful husband. As a mob fearing Catholic, she couldn't leave him, so – – this is so hard to say.

MALAISE. Of course it is. But you'll feel so much better if you get it out.

FATHER. I think Toffee put the contract on her own husband. – There, I did it. I accused the woman I love.

MALAISE. Now, doesn't that feel better?

FATHER. No.

MALAISE. Well then, it will in an hour. (*To* **TOFFEE**) Now Toffee, its your turn. Don't hold back. Just let it loose.

TOFFEE. Alright (*She jumps at* **FATHER** *and starts hitting him*) You two-faced celibate tease!

MALAISE. Toffee! Toffee! We don't do that here. We don't get our aggressions out that way. We either talk them out or shoot them out. But not with fists.

(**TOFFEE** *stops.* **TONY** *has begin to watch* **MALAISE** *contemplatively. Through out the rest of the scene,* **TONY** *watches her and begins to figure it all out.*)

TOFFEE. You're right. I'm sorry.

MALAISE. Don't apologize to me, apologize to the group.

TOFFEE. I'm sorry everybody.

MALAISE. Now what does everyone say to Toffee?

EVERYONE. Forget about it!

MALAISE. Good – now, Toffee – maybe it would help if you put your feelings into words?

TOFFEE. I'll try. First I feel betrayed.

MALAISE. (*writing*) Betrayed – good. Go on.

TOFFEE. Yes, maybe I have been dissatisfied with the way my life with Tony has turned out. Especially as I've been under the constant criticism of his mother, Nona. And how Tony won't open his eyes and see her for what she really is.

MALAISE. Good, now we're getting somewhere, Toffee. And in your eyes, what is Mrs. Nona Alto – besides your mother-in-law?

TOFFEE. A crazy, self centered, hateful person. A woman so mad at the world that she's turned that anger against her own son. I think she put the contract out on Tony. She even said she had the phone number right next to her phone. She's mentally unstable.

MALAISE. (*writing*) So you see her as a dangerous force?

TOFFEE. Have you ever seen her at the dinner table? Believe me, she is a dangerous force!

MALAISE. Mrs. Alto – Nona. What is your reaction to what your daughter-in-law has just said?

NONA. Bite your tongue and choke on it.

MALAISE. Alright. Now that you've gotten that out – what are your thoughts?

NONA. My thoughts? I have so many – they're always running around in my head, bumping into each other, pushing each other – talking with funny voices. Sometimes the voice is coming from my neighbors dog. I don't know my own thoughts no more. My brother – he's to blame. He's the one always talking about how the new generation don't have no respect. He's the one who kept talking about killing my Tony. He's the one that gave me that number! (*Pointing to* **UNCLE SENIOR**) Look at him – a bitter man, never given his turn to run things. That bitterness is a poison. He's the one – he's the one that hired those thugs to rub out my only son Tony.

MALAISE. Good. Very good Nona.

(**NONA** *smiles, a little embarrassed.*)

MALAISE. Everyone, didn't Nona do well this time?

(*Everyone applauds.* **NONA** *smiles sheepishly, then the smile drops – .*)

NONA. Bite your tongue and choke on it!

MALAISE. Alright. Now it's your turn uncle Senior. You've heard your sister opening up and telling her side. Why don't you open up and share with the group.

UNCLE SENIOR. The group – this group don't know no respect!

MALAISE. (*writing*) Good start – now keep going.

UNCLE SENIOR. All of you – none of you know – none of you could understand! It was my turn – my turn to run things and then (*pointing to* **TONY**) He took it all away. And what did I get? (*Pointing to the anklets, bracelets, etc.*) These – these are what I got! Okay – okay – so I wanted my nephew Tony dead! Big deal! Who hasn't wanted a member of their family dead? (*To person in audience*) You know what I mean, right?

MALAISE. They'll have their turn later. Right now we're concentrating on you, Uncle Senior.

UNCLE SENIOR. Right. Sorry. But it wasn't me that put that hit on Tony. I didn't have the guts – or the cash actually. No, it was Tony's own right hand that betrayed him. It was that little rat Chris that was selling us all out so he could become a made man – in Hollywood. But Tony forbid him, even though Chris had already signed with HBO. That was his dream Tony was taking away. I know – I know what it's like to have your dream stolen away. You'd kill if it would make a difference. And Chris is good at that.

MALAISE. Good – Uncle Senior. Now we're to you Tony. After all, this has all been about you.

TONY. Yeah, doc, I know.

MALAISE. Well, Tony. What are your thoughts – your feelings on what has been said here tonight?

TONY. I – I have to thank you doc – 'cause I think I'm beginning to see things more clearly.

MALAISE. (*writing*) Good, good. Now we might be getting somewhere. Go on.

TONY. Yeah – I think I see the whole picture now. It's like you said – how if I step back and try and look at things objectively – how everything will come into focus.

MALAISE. And what has come into focus?

TONY. Who it was that put the hit on me. I can see it clearly now! I left straight from your office to the motel. So whoever it was had to have known I was seeing you. They had to have been waiting outside your office to follow me there. But the real eye opener for me was when that first shooter showed up here tonight. He arrived maybe five minutes after I interrupted the Fathers ceremony to reveal that I wasn't dead like everyone was thinking. Five whole freakin minutes! How could he have gotten here so fast? Who could have called him? Most nobody left the room in that time, and even if they had they didn't have no time to call the Krays, tell them where I was and for the Krays to pack it and get over here. Not in five minutes. Before Father Flips ceremony, everyone thought I was dead – except one person that is. But what I don't get is (*To* **MALAISE**) why'd you want me dead, Doc?

MALAISE. Tony? You don't know what you're saying. I think your Prozac has run out. Here – I think I have one for you.

TONY. You were the one person I talked to the moment I first arrived at my own wake, a good twenty minutes before Father Flip started his ceremony.

MALAISE. (*digging for pills*) Tony, I think maybe we need to put you back on the Lithium.

TONY. You worked extra hard tonight to made sure every-one else's motives were brought to light.

(**CHRIS** *pulls out his gun and steps towards her.*)

MALAISE. Tony – you can't seriously be thinking that I –

TONY. This is hard for me too, Doc. But you were the only person who had enough time to make a call to the Krays. The only one. Why, Doc, why?

MALAISE. WHY? Why do you think why? Do you really need to ask me why? (*She swallows some pills herself*). You've ruined my life is why! –

(*Music starts.* **MALAISE** *sings a rock & roll song* **"BAD FOR ME"**)

"BAD FOR ME"

(*Rock & Roll style*)

YOU'VE GOT ME TOSSIN' AND TURNING
I NEVER SLEEP
YOU'VE GOT ME SADDLED WITH SECRETS
I'D BETTER KEEP
I GOT AN EYE ON THE CLOCK
AND ONE ON THE DOOR
'CAUSE I DON'T KNOW WHO MIGHT KNOCK
AND I DON'T KNOW WHAT FOR
I CAN'T GO ON LIVIN' THIS WAY
YOU'VE GOT TO SEE
BECAUSE YOU'RE BAD FOR MY BUSINESS
AND YOU'RE BAD FOR ME

YOU'VE GOT ME JUMPIN' AND TWISTIN'
AND LOOKIN 'ROUND
'CAUSE I'M AFRAID I MIGHT END
SIX FEET UNDERGROUND
YOU'VE GOT MY CLIENTS AND FRIENDS
TREMBLIN' IN THEIR SHOES
AND I'M SO MAD, I SEE RED
YET I'VE GOT THE BLUES
I SHOULD HAVE KNOWN FROM THE START
THIS WAS GONNA BE

A LOUSY DEAL FOR MY BUSINESS
AND SO BAD FOR ME

I TRIED TO EXTRICATE MYSELF FROM THE
SITUATION
BUT MY OPTIONS WERE MIGHTY FEW
I'M NOT A VIOLENT WOMAN
BUT I DO HAVE MY LIMITS
NOW WHAT WAS I SUPPOSED TO DO?

(**CHRIS** and **TONY** *start swaying behind her, like a 50's
back up group, snaping their fingers.*)

YOU HAD ME WISHIN' AND PRAYIN'
YOU WOULDN'T SHARE
I HAD SOME QUESTIONS TO ASK
BUT I DIDN'T DARE
I FEARED THE DAY WE WOULD MEET
IN A PUBLIC PLACE
I ONLY HOPED I COULD HIDE
OR AVERT MY FACE
YOU MIGHT HAVE THOUGHT IT WAS ENOUGH
THAT YOU PAID MY FEE
BUT YOU WERE TOO BAD FOR BUSINESS
YOU WERE BAD FOR ME

THE DAY I THOUGHT I WAS LOSING MY MIND
IT WAS CLEAR
THAT SOMETHING HAD TO BE DONE
TO MAKE YOU DISAPPEAR
I SIMPLY ACTED PROFESSIONALLY
TO KEEP THE BAD FROM MY BUSINESS
AND THE BAD, BAD MAN FROM ME.

(**CHRIS** *grabs her by the arm, pointing the gun at her.
She smiles, scared.*)

DR. MALAISE. Good night.

(*Black out. Gun shots. Bow music. Spot up for curtain
call. Winners announced, prizes given out. Bow music
plays out as cast exits.*)

FIN

MOVIE FILM TITLES IN SCRIPT (20)

Godfather
Goodfellas
Sopranos
Law & Order
NYPD Blue
Wiseguys
The whole nine yards.
Miller's Crossing
Married to the Mob
Mickey Blue Eyes
Analyze This
Pulp Fiction
Scarface
Little Ceasar
Once upon a Time in America
Pritzi's Honor
Donnie Brasco
Casino
The Krays
The Mexican

PROPS

Blackjack set-up
Craps set-up (with rigged dice)
Funeral Urn
Funeral Wreath
Photo of Tony
Ink blots
Cell phone
Electronic collar, bracelet and anklet (for Uncle Senior)
Pill contains
Ring box
Dog biscuit
Note pad & pencil
Flower bouquet with working gun
Long flower box with machine gun
5 working guns (Chris, Tony, Uncle Senior, Nona, Toffee)
Ace Bandage

Also by
David Landau & Nikki Stern...

Contempt of Court

Murder at Café Noir

Murderous Crossings

Noir Suspicious

Please visit our website **samuelfrench.com** for complete
descriptions and licensing information